Who put that there?

An Ivy and Mack story

T0337046

Written by Juliet Clare Bell

Illustrated by Gustavo Mazali

with Dusan Pavlic

Collins

What's in this story?

Listen and say

clue

treasure

Ivy and Mack were at Luke and Emma's house. It was a wet day.

"There's nothing to do, Aunt Libby!" said Ivy.

"Yes, there is," smiled Aunt Libby. "Come with me to the kitchen."

"What is it?" asked Ivy.

"I know!" said Emma.
"It's a treasure clue!"

"Do we get treasure at the end?"
asked Mack.

"Here is clue number one," said Aunt Libby. "Go to the living room. Count to 50. Then read the clue."

Ivy, Mack, Luke and Emma ran into the living room. They counted to 50. Luke read the clue.

In this room, you learn to cook.
Where's the clue? Look in the book ...

Luke and Ivy looked at each other. "The kitchen," they said.

Emma looked up at the books. "The cookbooks!" she said.

"I can get them!" said Luke.

"Which is Mum's favourite book?" asked Mack.

"This one," said Luke.

Luke read clue number two.

Climb the stairs and look for pink.
When you find it, have a drink ...

"Let's go," said Ivy.

There were some flowers on the stairs.
Mack picked one up.

"These pink flowers are nice!" said Mack.

"They're in the clue, Mack!" said Luke.
"*Look for pink ...*"

They found a box.

"*Have a drink?*" thought Mack. "I know! We drink from a cup!"

"This is exciting," said Emma.

Ivy read the new clue.

I have lots of pictures and lots of words.
Do you like my red birds?

Emma jumped up and down. "My favourite book has red birds in it!"

I get wet. You get dry. What am I?
read Luke.

"*I get wet?*" thought Ivy. "You get wet in the bathroom! Let's look in there!"

Mack played with Emma's frog and got wet.

"Mack! Dry your hands and help us find the next clue," said Ivy.

She gave Mack a towel. "Look!" said Emma.

"The *towel* gets wet ... and ... *you* get dry!" said Ivy.

It was the next clue.

Emma read the new clue.
You're doing well. You found this clue!
Find Luke's favourite thing – the treasure
is there, too!

"Let's go to Luke's room," said Mack.

Ivy and Mack ran to Luke's room. "What's your favourite thing, Luke?" asked Mack.

"I know! And it's not in his room!" laughed Emma.

They ran to the cupboard under the stairs.
"Luke's favourite thing is his *skateboard*!"
said Emma.

"Is the clue on the skateboard?"
asked Mack.

Emma tried to get the skateboard out of
the cupboard.

A pretty old box fell down. Luke caught it.
"Wow!" he said. "Who put that there?"

Ivy laughed. "Aunt Libby did!
It's the treasure!"

They took the treasure to the living room. It was chocolate. Aunt Libby came into the room. "Now then! Who found the treasure?"

"I did!" said Emma.

"It's yummy treasure," said Mack.

"Well done!" said Aunt Libby. "And there's a ticket for the cinema for everyone, too!"

"I love wet days at Luke and Emma's house," Ivy said to Mack. "There are always lots of things to do!"

Picture dictionary

Listen and repeat

cinema

cookbook

skateboard

towel

1 Look and order the story

2 Listen and say

Collins

Published by Collins
An imprint of HarperCollins*Publishers*
Westerhill Road
Bishopbriggs
Glasgow
G64 2QT

HarperCollins*Publishers*
1st Floor, Watermarque Building
Ringsend Road
Dublin 4
Ireland

William Collins' dream of knowledge for all began with the publication of his first book in 1819.

A self-educated mill worker, he not only enriched millions of lives, but also founded a flourishing publishing house. Today, staying true to this spirit, Collins books are packed with inspiration, innovation and practical expertise. They place you at the centre of a world of possibility and give you exactly what you need to explore it.

10 9 8 7 6 5 4 3 2

ISBN 978-0-00-839671-8

Collins® and COBUILD® are registered trademarks of HarperCollins*Publishers* Limited

www.collins.co.uk/elt

British Library Cataloguing in Publication Data

A catalogue record for this publication is available from the British Library.

Author: Juliet Clare Bell
Lead illustrator: Gustavo Mazali (Beehive)
Copy illustrator: Dusan Pavlic (Beehive)
Series editor: Rebecca Adlard
Commissioning editor: Zoë Clarke
Publishing manager: Lisa Todd
Product managers: Jennifer Hall and Caroline Green
In-house editor: Alma Puts Keren
Project manager: Emily Hooton
Editor: Deborah Friedland
Proofreaders: Natalie Murray and Michael Lamb
Cover designer: Kevin Robbins
Typesetter: 2Hoots Publishing Services Ltd
Audio produced by id audio, London
Reading guide author: Julie Penn
Production controller: Rachel Weaver
Printed and bound by: GPS Group, Slovenia

MIX
Paper from
responsible sources
FSC
www.fsc.org
FSC™ C007454

This book is produced from independently certified FSC™ paper to ensure responsible forest management.

For more information visit: **www.harpercollins.co.uk/green**

Download the audio for this book and a reading guide for parents and teachers at www.collins.co.uk/839671